One, two, three, four, five...

Bear turned the corner and went to the sink.

He combed his whiskers. He washed his paws.

He brushed his teeth.

Finally, with a big yawn, he climbed into bed.
But...

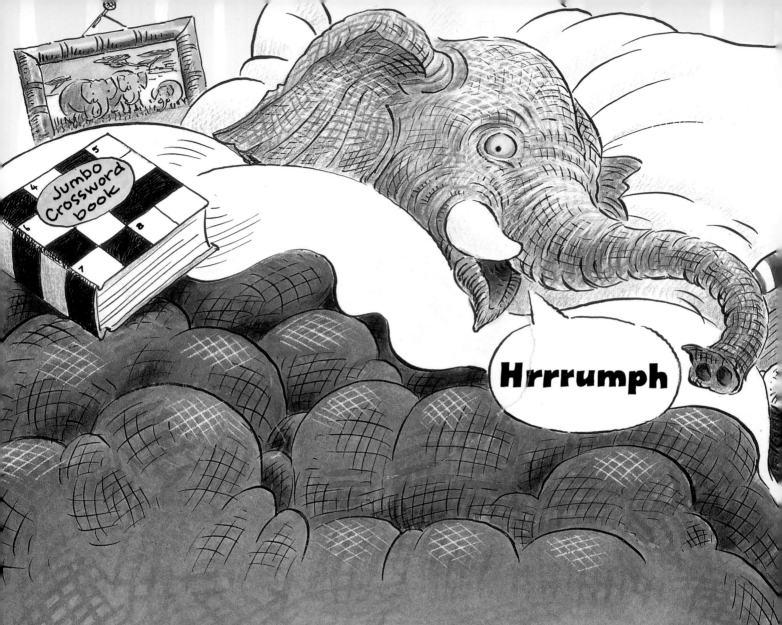

"Hey!" said Bear. "This isn't my bed. It's big and bumpy, wrinkly and lumpy. It's Elephant's bed!"

"Where's my bed?" he wondered. "Ah! There it is."
And he crossed the room and crawled under the
covers. Bear was very sleepy.
But...

Don't
forget!

"Oh, no!" said Bear. "This isn't my bed.
It's eency-weency, teeny-weeny. And it squeaks.
It's Mouse's bed!"

EEK! EEK!

CHEESES OF THE WORLD

Tales of Terror!

"There's my bed!" Bear said. And he shuffled across the room and burrowed under the blankets. But...

"Goodness gracious!" said Bear. "This isn't my bed. It's hard and knobbly, long and wobbly. It's Crocodile's bed!"

GRRRRR

WATER SPORTS

"There's my bed!" Bear said. And he tiptoed across the room and slipped under the quilt. But...

"Help!" said Bear. "This isn't my bed. It's lanky and lofty, spindly and spotty. It's Giraffe's bed!"

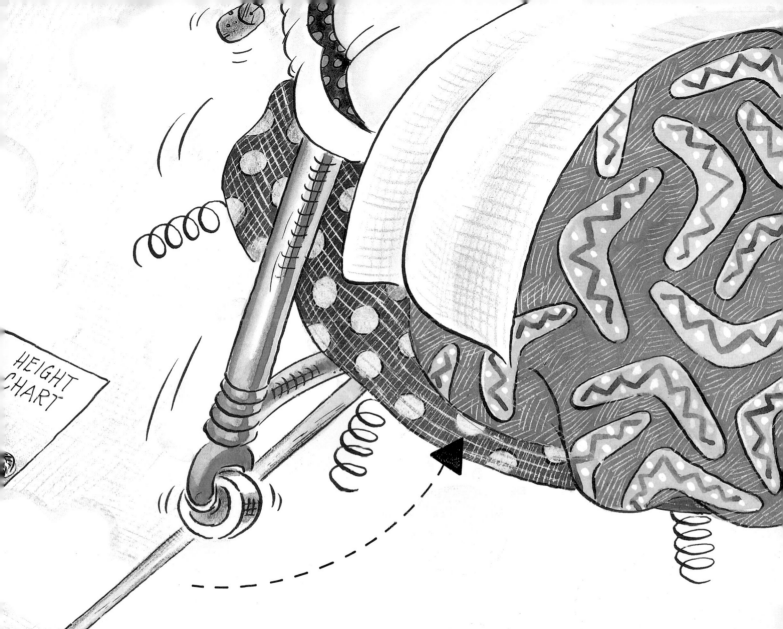

"There's my bed!" he said. And Bear crept across
the room and climbed under the comforter.
But...

"Whoops!" said Bear. "This is definitely not my bed. It's bouncy and flouncy, prancy and dancy. It's Kangaroo's bed!"

So Bear hopped off the bed and slipped through the door.
And...

"Ah!" said Bear. "THERE'S my bed. It's cozy
and cuddly, soft and snoozy, fleecy and friendly,
and just right for me.
It's my bed!"

So Bear climbed into his bed, snuggled down,
and turned off the light...